.THE
pigeon
MEN

Felicity McCall

eve

eve is an imprint of Guildhall Press dedicated to encouraging, promoting and showcasing the creativity of women authors and artists.

Published in March 2014

Guildhall Press
Unit 15, Ráth Mór Business Park
Bligh's Lane,
Derry, BT48 0LZ
Ireland
(028) 7136 4413
info@ghpress.com • www.ghpress.com

Guildhall Press gratefully acknowledges the financial support of the Arts Council of Northern Ireland as a principal funder under its Annual Funding Programme.

Acknowledgements

My gratitude to: the Arts Council of Northern Ireland for continuing support and encouragement; Paul Hippsley, Declan Carlin, Jenni Doherty, Joe McAllister, Kevin Hippsley and all at Guildhall Press for the highest standards of professional guidance and excellence; all those who shared the journey, and their soul, with me; my fellow writers, theatre practitioners, artists/activists and loved ones, who each, in their unique way, sustain me through the intensity of writing; and for Aoife, always.

About the Author

Felicity McCall is a career journalist turned full-time writer and occasional arts facilitator, theatre producer, actor and director of three theatre companies. Born in South Armagh, she has lived for half her life in Derry and Donegal. An Arts Council of NI Individual Artist award winner on seven occasions, she has also been awarded the Tyrone Guthrie prize for stage and screenplay writing and has two Meyer Whitworth nominations. Her published works include novels, non-fiction, young adult fiction, graphic novels, a dozen plays for the professional stage and four screenplay credits. Her work has travelled across Europe, Australasia and the USA. More information is available on: www.felicitymccall.com

Also by Felicity McCall
with Guildhall Press

A Pitying of Doves
Finding Lauren
Agnes Jones
Reckoning

For survivors,
everywhere

Chapter 1

The Present

THERE ARE FORTY PLASTER ROSES DEFINING the rectangle of the courtroom ceiling. If you count them another way, you get forty-four, but that's incorrect. There are fourteen on the ceiling above me, stretching from the high barred window at one end to the polished oak platform where the judge sits at the other. Fourteen parallel on the opposite side, above the security guards and the public gallery and where the jury should be. But there is no jury today. They have been discharged. The man in the dock has changed his plea. It's a deal, though deals do not, of course, exist in the Northern Ireland courts of law. He has spared his victims the ordeal of giving evidence in the hope of leniency, a shorter sentence. Across the judge's platform and above the barred window hang two matching rows of eight identical roses. Forty-four. I have been counting them for fourteen months, three weeks and two days. Not on a daily basis, you understand, just when

I'm here. Physically. And when my mind wants to be somewhere else. But it's really only forty, as the corner roses can only be counted once, can only be included in one tally. It doesn't make any difference as long as you remember not to count them twice. You have to be accurate. Get the facts straight. That's important, in a courtroom.

It's quite calming, counting the ceiling roses, watching the glowing globe lights suspended from them gently sparkling the dust cloud high above our heads.

It stops me thinking.

I'm fine with looking, though. Looking is OK. All picture and no sound we used to call it when Auntie Vee was throwing a strop. That's what I've made him. The accused. The protagonist in his own silent movie.

There's a roll of flabby white belly hanging over the waist of his grey striped polyester suit trousers. Lavender shirt, damp patches the size of a side plate under each arm. Navy polyester tie, with a discreet lavender stripe. His suit jacket is folded on the bench beside him. I imagine I can smell its odour, dried sweat mixed with the sourness of an ulcerated stomach. Cheap acrid aftershave and stale smoke.

His pale blue eyes are glazed, bloodshot, focussed on infinity. The sparse, sandy comb-over is damp with sweat, too. Sweat trickles down his puffy cheeks, over the broken capillaries splashed dark red and on to his fleshy lips. His bottom lip is bleeding. Just a little. Has he been chewing it? He is mumbling to himself. A prayer? A denial? A plea for forgiveness? What is your inarticulate litany?

I see his nails are bitten to the quick, the skin at the side of them torn away, raw. He picks at the hangnails. Sometimes they bleed, too. Just a little.

The judge is speaking. He has been speaking for more than an hour now. It is a long summing-up, even by the standards of Court Four. He has much to consider, he says. Victim impact reports. Character references. Probation reports. Things must be weighed in the balance. I have nothing to consider because I choose not to listen. That's not quite accurate. I choose to listen in a detached, objective way until my mind buzzes with the clichéd observation of the bitter: that the accused's victims have no choice over the duration of their sentence, or its severity. Life means life. I feel my legs shake. That's when I stop listening and start counting the lights. Again. They never change. The comfort of ritual.

The public gallery is less than half-full. I watch the man in the dock's family. On the right, nearest the door, the unbelievers. Those who say his accusers are only out for the money, for revenge, that what's past is past, that it was different times, a different world. Those who see only the beloved son, uncle, cousin, brother. They have been brought up to believe that blood is thicker than water. Yet the same blood flows through the veins of those whose accusations have brought him to this place. They sit, close together, within touching distance of the PSNI support team, the prison officers, the social services representatives, the charity volunteers.

There are eleven of them and seventeen of the others.

Is that what they call a majority verdict?

Those numbers change, though. Some days there have been fewer than half a dozen on each side of the invisible moral barrier. Not everyone can stand the pace, especially if they don't just look but choose to listen. Twice there has been no-one. That's because the judge has cleared the court. No-one to hear accusations and denials, evidence and counter-evidence. But today there is no drama, no mystery. No evidence. The man in the dock is guilty as charged. His legal team has said so. And now the judge must consider many, many things before he decides what to do with him. He will have to sign the Sex Offenders' Register, be returned to custody to await sentence, meet his probation officer, draw up a plan for his rehabilitation.

I know quite a lot about this, for a lay person. No, I know a lot. Because I have been here too often and it is always different yet always the same. The terminology changes when the plea changes. The alleged victims are now the victims. I choose to call us survivors, but that's me. We know each other from our empty eyes. In the street, the classroom, the workplace, wherever life takes us. Or we take ourselves. The pub, the therapy sessions, the hospital. We know each other by instinct, by some primeval wisdom, even if we choose not to acknowledge each other, for some pain is too personal to be shared. We cherish our isolation. Maybe that's what we recognise – the incalculable loneliness, the isolation. No-one else sees it. But we do. I do.

But I am thinking too much. And thinking can be dangerous. Better to be listening. Properly listening. But to tell you the truth, Judge, I'm not that interested. I don't really care. It's irrelevant. Family man, good work record, years of service, regular churchgoer, respected member of the community. Heard it all before. Until one thing registers.

Just the one.

I think it comes under the broad scope of character references and mitigating circumstances.

'… served as secretary of the local racing pigeon association for the past twenty-seven years …'

That's why it all seems so familiar.

So soul-chillingly, darkly familiar.

He's one of them.

The Pigeon Men.

Chapter 2

The Past

'DID YOUR GRANDA LIKE HIS PRESENTS?'

Carrie stands in the doorway that leads from the gloom of the hall to the front parlour, the good room, opened in honour of the season, though the blinds remain drawn to the street. It is the middle of a December afternoon and the shortest day has yet to come, before the year turns. The only light is from the reproduction Victorian globes on their gilt brackets, the twisted cones of their twin bulbs reflecting on the plastic shroud that has protected the dark brown three-piece suite since it arrived from the showroom and which sticks to the back of your thighs when you sit on it and makes you sweaty. The silver and green artificial tree remains decorated from year to year under its plastic dust cover. It will be removed on Christmas morning when the tree lights and the teardrop chandelier in the middle of the ceiling will be kept switched on all day. So will the electric fire that stands in the bricked-up fireplace. For now, all is dark. Deep red flock wallpaper, dark brown velvet curtains, the two colours mixed in great swirls and arcs in the fitted carpet.

The adults sit in this early dusk, arrayed in awkward poses along the sofa and in the matching chairs and on the dark red chaise longue. The sofa is too deep for their legs; they are not a tall family. Her da sits hunched forward on the edge of his cushion, feet planted firmly on the carpet in front of him. Her mam sits with her spine pressed into the back of the sofa and when she forgets, she tucks up her stockinged feet under herself for comfort. She will do this more as the afternoon drags on and more drinks are poured, more lives dissected. Her grown-up cousins Craig and Sharon and her Uncle Ron and her Auntie Vee and Sharon's husband, Alex, make up the tableau: an extended family enjoying a Christmas drink.

Carrie becomes aware of the silence.

'Dolly daydream,' Vee casts her eyes to heaven as Sharon nods her agreement. 'Away with the birds. Answer your mother.'

What was the question again?

Did your granda like his presents?

She cannot answer because there is no answer.

Her mam looks at her, encouraging, willing her to be civil. To be normal. Not to show her up in company.

'I think so. Yes, he did.' She hears her voice before she realises that she has answered. It is meaningless but, it seems, it will suffice.

13

Craig switches on the big twenty-four inch television in the corner and she shuffles over to sit in front of it. The volume must be kept low – just loud enough to drown out the substance of the grown-up conversation.

She is aware of Vee's pointed comment to her mam that the child would be better off out in the kitchen with one of her books. Those books that her head is never out of, this strange child. Craig and Sharon never bothered with books. Vee does not hold with reading or too much in the way of education. She says it makes people get above themselves. Carrie knows 'people' means her. And her mam and da. She knows her mam and da will defend her. She has seen Vee burning books on the bonfire out the back. Hitler burned books. It is Vee who is strange, but the rest of them don't seem to realise it.

'The old bastard has been lying in his bed these three days and he has me wore out running up and down the stairs to him.' Vee is never happy.

Someone, her soft-spoken da most likely, has asked about her father's health. The man has outlived his allocated span of three-score years and ten and with it his daughter's tolerance. The brown envelopes her da brings her every time he visits, the ones that annoy her mam, seem to help Vee's nerves. Just a little.

Carrie does not want to hear any more. She would rather read in the kitchen but she has only brought one book. She is halfway through it and she is saving the rest in case the afternoon runs into evening. Because then something like *The Benny Hill Show* will come on the TV with its lithe-legged girls with long, long per-oxide blonde hair and eyelashes like the fringes on the wall lamps and Vee will lose the plot and switch it off in disgust, screeching words they don't use at home and possibly cuffing Ron round the ear or bursting into copious weeping. Best to save a few chapters. Or tell herself stories from the book inside her head. The one nobody else can see.

There is a cartoon featuring cheeky mice, teasing a slow-witted and slothful cat. Sooner or later her da will comment that the cartoons are great value altogether and her mam will reply that the ads are better than some of the programmes that are on. They are newfan-gled with these, as only Ron and Vee have ITV. Their older set does not. Her da thinks you can trust the BBC news and one channel is enough for anybody. Still, Carrie wouldn't mind a three-channel set from Radio Rentals like lots of her friends have. Then she could join in the conversations about *Crossroads* and *Coronation Street,* instead of being strange.

The *Benny Hill* girls are lovely, Carrie thinks. Her mam and da do not. Carrie would love to be tall and leg-gy and to look great in knee-length boots and hot pants and polo necks and to have waved peroxide blonde hair and long painted nails and a face clattered with make-up. Instead she has rolls of marbled, pockmarked fat on her thighs that rub together and chafe. Her tummy sticks out too much to wear anything but smock dresses which her mam sews for her and, if she could, she would keep her coat on all the time. It is puppy fat, she has been told, and it will go away in time, but she wishes it would go now. She knows it keeps her at her books, as she is not cut out for socialising and there will be plenty of time for that when she leaves home to go to university to study to be a doctor or a lawyer or a bilingual secretary with a job in Brussels, which is where her da says the future will be. For now, she wishes that a doctor would cut her open from knee to crotch and from hip to hip and suck away all the handfuls of lumpy, lardy fat. All the patches of discoloured skin where her thighs have rubbed together. Suck out all the hard red pulsing boils that throb in the night, the open sores that her mam covers with paste and lint to draw out the pus. And then sew her up again. A new person. A thin one. A normal one. Who didn't live her life in her head.

She is aware of raised voices, of dissent. She tries not to listen to what they are saying.

She wishes she could ask her mam to buy her a bra. She knows she needs one. The girls at school have told her so. They don't understand why she can't just go up the town on a Saturday to the department store and get fitted for one. They do lovely teenage bras, with blue and lavender or pink and orange flowers. Her mam would choose pink and orange. Carrie tells the girls that her family goes visiting every weekend to give a hand with her granda, as her Aunt Vee suffers from her nerves.

She knows she needs a bra because her granda had pulled at her veined and droopy breasts and told her she is 'getting real woman'. And it had hurt, even through her clothes. He had pinched the nipples, and that had been really sore. It had brought tears to her eyes. And Carrie does not cry.

Behind her, Craig has gone to the reproduction teak-veneer drinks cabinet and brought an armful of bottles to the coffee table. He plays the dutiful host, refilling glasses against half-hearted protests. Port and brandy for Vee. Soon, she will be admonishing them all to shut up while she sings. Mam detests port and brandy. She has told Carrie this. Mam will have a sherry. Her da is on whiskey and Craig and Sharon and Alex are on Bacardi and Coke, which is fashionable, and tastes like ordinary Coke, except when you sip it it makes your head giddy and you feel all warm and glowing inside. And happy. And safe from the world, just like when you escape into the stories in your head. The drink shields you. Nothing can touch you. Carrie knows this because Craig has let her taste it when he sneaked her out to the loft to see Granda's pigeons. She does not like them much. The dust and the fluff and the frightening power of holding the frail, pulsing birds in her hand, sensing how easily she could crush them. Craig keeps his own bottle in the pigeon loft away from what he calls 'thieving hands', and he encourages her to giggle about this. He is proposing she collude in a shared secret. Soon, she suspects, he will offer her more. More secrets. Perhaps Craig likes her. Perhaps he feels sorry for her, the fat, ungainly child who reads away her days.

'What age is she now?' she hears Vee asking her father.

No-one asks her. Why would they? She is twelve. Next year she will be thirteen. A teenager. In five years, six at the most, she will have escaped to live her life. Provided she keeps her head in the books and keeps herself to herself. Stays strange.

'Sure she's old enough. Give her a proper one, there.'

That's Vee. No-one argues with Vee when she has drink taken. Vee is highly strung. She suffers from nerves. And she has to look after Granda, who has lived beyond his time. Vee does her duty.

Craig squeezes her shoulder as he hands her the cut-crystal tumbler filled to the brim and Vee screeches at her not to set it on the floor in case she knocks it over and spills it on the carpet. So she clutches it with both hands, so tightly the crystal is in danger of cracking and slicing her fingers. Carrie takes comfort in the pain of the diamond-cut facets pressing into her soft palms. She swallows and realises at once that there is a lot of Bacardi in the Coke. A lot. More than before.

It tastes of almonds and coconut and exotic and grown-up and escape. She sips again. Soon it has guided her ever so gently into today's story, where Carrie is seventeen, with long dancer's legs and peroxide tresses and manicured nails and perfect teeth and a cross-your-heart bra that makes her chest go out, not down. And where her granda no longer rubs his big knobbly fingers up and down the crotch of her knickers and pulls her breasts till they hurt and thrusts his big slobbery tongue down her throat and kneads his toothless gums into hers. And laughs. Deep, throaty laughs and stares her straight in the eyes as he does it. And all because she was sent to his room to give him his Christmas presents. But it was OK because by then, Carrie – the real Carrie – was long gone. Safe inside her head. Where no-one else can go without her permission.

CHAPTER 3

The Past

THE PIGEON LOFT IS MEN'S TERRITORY, AS much as the funeral cortège or the public bar or the Masonic Hall. Men and, occasionally, children. Chosen children. Women do not go there, even though it is only a few hundred yards away from the back door, beyond the rotating washing line and beside the dilapidated shed that is crammed with spare furniture, old curtains, bundles of newspapers, all infused with the warm earthy smell of the Bramley apples that are stored there each winter. The shed is locked.

'Your pigeon has been domesticated since Biblical times,' her granda expounds, the first time he takes Carrie down the garden to show her the loft. She is eight. They have just started to visit Granda and his family again. They had been estranged for years, or, in her mam's opinion, 'not bloody long enough'. It was because of one of the things grown-ups talked about when children were watching the cartoons or reading in the kitchen. Carrie has no idea why the visits had stopped when she was a toddler. Before she remembered them. Or why they have started again, just as inexplicably. Carrie knows that Auntie Vee feels hard done by because she lives with Granda all the time and she suffers from nerves, and everyone, especially her da, seems so pleased that Granda, who can be a grumpy old bastard, has taken to his youngest grandchild. Her. Her da is with them, that day, in the garden, but he has heard all the old stories before and is weary of them, impatient to be back in the house with Mam.

Carrie senses it is an honour, a gift, to be allowed into the loft. It is dark and dusty and the air makes her throat tickle so she keeps coughing little dry hacking coughs.

'Your man with a bad chest, your asthmatic, can't go near them,' Granda continues to share his wisdom. 'Vee thinks they carry TB. Her arse. You're a grand healthy girl. You've a bit of weight to fall back on.'

'Better that than too thin,' her da cuts in. 'You need a bit of reserve.'

To mention TB is to invoke a curse on the family home. Vee spent almost two years in the TB hospital where she had lost any weight she might once have carried, and acquired her nerves and a forty-a-day habit that exacerbated her cough. She shuns the loft. Uncle Ron is more into the rallying but he sometimes feigns an interest in the pigeons in order to escape from the womenfolk.

Carrie doesn't like the claustrophobic, dank atmosphere of the loft, the feathers that seem forever floating in the dusty air, the sickly smell of the pigeon feed that reminds her of stagnant pond water. She knows the pigeons are well cared for, but to her, their bedding stinks of stale urine. Sharp blades of straw scrape her fingers and the wire mesh tacked over the boards cuts into the soft fleshy pads beside her knees as she moves about while her granda catalogues each bird's progress. Craig, he says, is becoming a great man for the pigeons. Craig will take over his flock when he dies. It's a fine interest for a young man, Granda enthuses. It keeps them away from the dance halls and the women. Out of the pub and off the streets.

Craig spends time in the garden, too. He has taken over the shed. That is why it is locked. Carrie thinks it would make a great retreat for when she comes to visit, but Craig says he needs it for his tools and things. Craig doesn't own a car and Carrie has never seen him working on an engine in her life but she thinks maybe he needs to get away from the womenfolk, too. He is nineteen now. And Auntie Vee, they agree, can be hard going.

'Pigeons used to carry messages in the first World War,' Carrie tells her parents on the way home. 'To and from the trenches. I asked Granda did he ever use pigeons to send messages when he was at the Western Front but he said no.'

'And what else did he tell you about his time at the Western Front?' her mam interjects sharply and she sees her da silence her with a look. Mam puts on her huffy face then and goes quiet, so Carrie continues her story. It has captured her imagination, the little birds navigating their way through the darkness with vital instructions and information strapped to their fragile legs. Flying for miles, unswerving, guided by the stars and their inner compass.

'Some of them got medals, you know,' she goes on. 'It was a special medal. The Dickin medal for bravery. There was this one pigeon, in France, that flew twenty-five miles with an injured leg and a head wound. It saved lives. It was called Cher Ami,' she adds. 'That's French for dear friend. It was a dear friend to the soldiers, wasn't it? Granda says when he—'

'That'll do, thank you.' Mam's voice is cold. Carrie knows what that means. Disapproval. No more questions, no more chatter. And Carrie is expected to work out for herself, at eight years old, what she has said that is so wrong. What unspoken family code has she breached? She hasn't been rude. Or cheeky. Or told a lie. She doesn't know. She never knows. If she says anything more, she knows her parents will exchange covert glances, then one will speak, and immediately the other will start to back them up, agreeing and confirming, talking over each other, and still she won't understand what she has done.

Carrie lies down on the back seat and pulls up her legs under her coat and disappears with the brave, wounded pigeon that is flying young men's secrets through the chilly French night, guided only by the light of the stars and its mystical inner compass.

Chapter 4

The Past

THE PIGEON LOFT FACES TO THE SOUTH WEST.
Your racing pigeon must be kept warm and dry, Granda
tells Carrie, if you want to get the best performance out
of them. Your pigeon is a hot-blooded creature. Does
she know what the human body temperature should
be? Carrie has learned this at school. It's thirty-seven
degrees Celsius. Easy-peasy. Your pigeon, Granda says,
is around forty-two degrees. 'Hot wee ladies,' and he
chuckles. No draughts. No damp. The open-meshed
wire of the floor of the loft is to keep their feet dry. It
cuts into Carrie's flesh as she kneels inside. She wrig-
gles but cannot get comfortable. They have to have the
best of good food, too, the pigeons. If you feed them
shit, that's what you get in return. He laughs again. 'Tell
your mammy that. If shit goes in one end it comes out
the other.' Granda is pleased with his joke. He offers
it to Carrie as a conspiracy between them, just as he
offers her the chance to say what she wants about her

parents, especially Mam. Carrie knows Mam does not much like Granda. Mam does not much like Auntie Vee and Craig and Sharon, either. She refers to Uncle Ron as Ron-God-help-him. After she has been drinking sherry at their house, she has told Carrie, in a rare moment of intimacy, that Ron is like herself. He had no idea what he was marrying into. Carrie thinks Mam would not have cared if they had never gone back to visit again, ever, but there are the brown envelopes to be delivered. Her da seems pleased that Granda has an interest in the pigeons, and is passing it on to her. Granda used to like Sharon, but now Sharon and he hardly acknowledge each other and Sharon says she hates pigeons and she hopes to God the fox gets a good run at them one night soon. Sharon doesn't like many people. She has never let Carrie try on her clothes or offered to lend her magazines, but then maybe she doesn't have any. Carrie's not even sure if Sharon likes Alex very much, because she has her own bedroom, with all the furniture painted white and a white nylon quilted bedspread and white pillows with frills round the edges and a soft white rug beside the bed that cries out to be stroked and petted like a kitten. The light shades are white and frilled, too, and the dressing table has a glass top and rows upon rows of perfume bottles, sprays, jewel boxes, tissues in a frilled cloth cover, and, right in the middle, a gold brush and comb, both adorned with little red stick-on plastic roses. The bed is buried under a pile of soft toys of every description. Lots of bears, mostly in pastel shades,

most at least two feet tall. Alex has bought her one every Christmas and birthday and anniversary since they
started going out with each other. Carrie thinks it is the
most beautiful room she has ever seen, straight out of a
magazine. It is a room for a film star. But she's not sure
about the animals.

Her teddy is small and golden brown. He doesn't
wear little dresses and bonnets. Sharon calls them her
babies. Sharon has no babies, but Carrie is wise enough
to know it's something you don't talk about. She would
like a second cousin to play with in this mausoleum of
adult repression, unsaid words, covert secrets, suspect-
ed lies and where someone seems to be always pouring
drinks.

'You're miles away.' Carrie feels her granda's grip on
the soft flesh of her forearm and it hurts. Just a little.
But it makes her afraid. He is smiling again. He has his
teeth in, both sets, and there is spittle dribbling from
the corner of his mouth. It is not a happy smile. 'Your
da was the same. Always with the head in a book, for all
the good it did him.'

It has done good, Carrie thinks. They are very proud
of her da, who got himself educated and wears a shirt
and tie to work and never smells of pigeon feed and
stale cigarettes. He doesn't have the acrid reek of stale
alcohol sweated through his skin, like Auntie Vee. Or
Craig. And sometimes Sharon, though she tries to hide
it with mouthwash and *Just Musk* perfume. Granda
doesn't smell of alcohol, either. He must have smelled

awful, years ago, but now he has put the cork in the bottle and the whole family is very happy and proud and his only vice is the fags which will only hurt himself, the ITV Seven, and the pigeons.

'Carrie! Car-o-line. Sweet Caroline.' He is gripping harder. There is something in his voice that makes her afraid but she does not know what it is and she feels foolish.

'Do you want to learn how to hold one? You'll have to hold tight. You can't let them get away …' he stares at her, '… or get at each other.'

It is Craig, poking his head into the loft. He is laughing, too. A helmet dangles from his right arm. Craig has been away but now he is back and he has bought a scooter. It's what her mam calls a 'wee phut phut'. He parks it beside the shed. She knows she is never to get on the back of it, no matter what he says.

Carrie doesn't understand what he means.

'They're not allowed to get at each other. They're separated in the spring.'

Craig looks at her as if she is simple.

'Did Granda not tell you?'

Carrie shakes her head.

'The males and the females. You keep them apart. For nine months of the year. Until the breeding season. No nookie.'

Carrie feels her cheeks burn. She tries to stop it by counting the rows of cages but it's no good.

Craig sees it and he knows.

'No fucking till the breeding season. Then you let them at each other. They're ready to tear each other apart by then. They fight the bit out. And then they mate.'

'You watch your language.' Granda feigns a clip on the ear but he is not angry. He is enjoying Carrie's discomfort.

'You come back here when we're breeding them, Carrie. They fuck like mad things. You want to see them.'

Carrie feels a pulse throbbing between her legs. She has a sudden urge to touch herself, to rub her finger up and down the crotch of her knickers. Why? What is happening? She wants to run out, but Craig and Granda are laughing and she wishes they would stop. If she runs out, they will laugh more. She takes a deep breath.

'Granda's teaching me to hold a pigeon.'

'Is he, now?'

She does not like the way Craig is looking at her. She feels his eyes move slowly across her chest, down to her stomach, and below. Why must she be so chubby? She is embarrassed by her size, by the assumptions it draws. She is greedy. She loves her sweeties. She is lazy. One night she found herself crying because she wanted a pair of jeans like the girls in her class and her mam soothed her and her da had appealed to her ma if that was what Carrie wanted, then why could they not get them for her? Were they *that* dear? But Da didn't understand that if Mam went to buy her jeans she would get them from some awful women's shop and they'd have an elasticated waist and they'd have to have yards taken off the legs and they would look ridiculous on her and they would never, ever, look like *Wrangler*s or *Levis* any more than she would ever look like a *Wrangler* or *Levis 501* poster girl. Not one inch of her face or body would ever look like that. Only in a very secret and special place in her mind might she aspire to it. It was almost beyond her power to conjure up that blissful image. She saved it for times of real desperation. It involved the doctor who would cut away and suck out her excess flesh, and suck out and drain the spots and blackheads, sores and boils that punctuated her flabby body from face to thigh. The fairy godmother who would get her teeth fixed, fit her for contact lenses, acrylic nails. Anyone who could make her normal. Anonymous. Carrie had no expectation that it would ever happen.

'You need to keep a firm grip on her.'

Granda's words drew her back from a better place, to the reality of dust and pigeon meal and stale urine.

'Like the women, Granda. Treat them mean, keep them keen,' Craig laughed as he strode off.

'Stay away from the women!' Granda called after him.

But Carrie knows Craig is going down the pub and that Auntie Vee will make him eat mints if he wants to ride his scooter afterwards so his breath won't smell if he gets stopped by the police.

Carrie squirms as Granda pours the pigeon into her cupped hands. She can feel its heartbeat as it struggles for freedom.

'Get the four fingers folded round her lower body. Like that.' Granda is tall. He leans over her, rubbing against her back, his bony arms circling her and the captive pigeon. 'Good girl. Now the other hand. Hold her on the breast with your thumb. Have you got the breast? It's soft and fleshy. And warm. Feel it. There. And keep her feet free. That's it. You're going nowhere now,' he laughs.

Which of us? Me or the pigeon?

Granda is rubbing hard against her. His body is pressing into hers and something is pushing into the gap between her fleshy buttocks. She hears him grunt. Deep, guttural grunts. She talks through her embarrassment.

'Why do they always come back?'

'It's home. They might struggle to get away – hold her tight now – but your pigeon will always come home.'

'Why?'

'Why wouldn't they? They know nothing else. It's home. It's too dangerous out there in the wild, with predators and foxes and the bad weather. The best specimens come back. It's called natural selection. The weak ones fall away. They get lost or they get killed. They die. But your champion pigeon will always come straight home. I knew a man said they have a thing called a magnetic flux inside them and it aligns itself with the earth's magnetic flux lines and that's what guides them home. Every time. It's Mother Nature at work. They always come back.'

Granda suddenly jerks away and Carrie almost drops the pigeon. He swears at her, grabs the frightened bird and thrusts it roughly back into its cage. He slides the bolt in place. On the way out he will lock the loft.

'Away inside to your mam and da. That'll do you for the day.'

He turns his back to her and she sees his hand goes to the fly front of his baggy dun-coloured trousers. There is a stain spreading around the zip. Has he wet himself? Old people do, sometimes, she knows.

'Get away inside!' There is pure venom in his voice. Carrie turns and runs. She hopes her cheeks will stop burning before she joins her mam and da in the kitchen and they ask her if she had fun.

CHAPTER 5

The Present

THE SECURITY OFFICER LOOKS POINTEDLY AT his watch and taps the face with his index finger. I meet his eyes, nod, pick up my raincoat and loop my bag over my right shoulder. He is anxious to be done, to lock up for the day. The fleets of legal cars will be making their way towards Belfast, a convoy of gleaming black tailed by a rainbow scattering of private vehicles, dispersing and scattering down the roads to home. The big white van is still parked out the back, waiting for its daily quota of the accused, the remanded, the sentenced. There is no-one here to count the ceiling roses and the light globes, to watch the slow revolution of the ornate black hands on the clock face above the judge's bench, but the room must be locked. Its secrets must be contained. Left untouched until we are back in the morning. Or the morning after, or the one after that, for the judge has called for a point of law to be investigated, a point of law is to be back in the morning. Or the morning after, for it must be thoroughly investigated, the arguments juxtaposed, debated, considered with sufficient gravitas. The judicial system must be seen to be fair.

I see it as another game of counting. Eight to twelve years for the indecent assaults, gross indecency, and the one hundred and thirty-two other offences the defendant's legal team have asked to be taken into consideration, for, we have been reminded throughout, these are specimen charges. It is too long ago. Memories fade. Children are young. It is impossible to remember with acute clarity the minutiae of exact time and date and location. Knock off two to four for the guilty plea, but not at the first available opportunity – maybe two. And the victim-impact report. The woman, we have been told, is now leading a full and productive life. She is a mother. By implication, then, she is consensually sexually active. She has a job. A husband. He knows about her past. He empathises. That's nice. Maybe another two off? And even more for the exemplary conduct we can expect from our prisoner nonces – and minus time already spent in remand – that leaves six months. Taking into account the good character references, the defendant could be out in weeks. *Will* be out in weeks.

Was it worth it, lady with the empathic husband and the full and productive life? I can't answer that, I can only answer for me. Will you be in court to hear justice meted out?

I won't.

For right now, I realise, I won't be back tomorrow or the day after or the one after that. Because I couldn't give a damn about what happens to the man in the dock. It's irrelevant. I've seen him, I've heard his truth. I've read his face.

And I have heard it confirmed in a court of law that he is a pigeon man. Another one for my collection. I'll let myself count them, soon. I deserve it. It's a grand big total, now.

CHAPTER 6

The Past

CARRIE WILL BE COMING TWELVE WHEN SHE sees her granda again. There has been a falling out, one that she is allowed to know has happened, but not why. It is not talked about. For the last two Christmases, she had signed a card and helped her mam wrap up a bottle of brandy, a bottle of sherry, a tin of Highland shortbread and a box of liqueur chocolates. Her da has delivered them along with the brown envelope he hands over to Auntie Vee every time he visits. She knows it contains money. Perhaps Auntie Vee is poor. Carrie suspects that both the shortbread and the chocolates may be unwanted gifts of theirs, going to a new home, but, as her mam says, it is the thought that counts and Carrie knows if her mam's thoughts were really allowed to count then a lump of coal in the toe of a stocking would be too good for them. The paper has been ironed to look new and the old Sellotape peeled off. Her mam says she wishes her da didn't have to make the drive all on his own, in this weather, but Carrie is astute enough by now to know this is not an invitation to explore the topic further. Instead, she and Mam bake mince pies in the kitchen, the range going full blast, and it's cosy and secure even if there is no bowl to lick like with a sandwich cake. No-one likes cold pastry off-cuts and the globs of suet in the sweet mince sticks in her teeth and tastes greasy and sour.

Carrie is older now and she worries more. She gets pains in her stomach at night. She can't get to sleep and then she is tired in the morning. She wishes someone would explain things to her, just once, and she would remember and not ask again. She does not know why they no longer visit but she senses it must be her fault. She does not know what she has done. And she worries. Her father comes back late at night. She hears voices from the kitchen. Not raised in anger, for that does not happen in Carrie's house; there is only silence. But urgent, animated. Something is not right.

In the morning when she is eating her porridge, her da tells her that one of Granda's pigeons has won a race. It flew home from France. Auntie Vee is to collect the trophy at the club's dinner dance. Carrie expects it will be a little plastic and silver column with a silver-plated pigeon on top. It's not a Dickin medal, but it's not bad at all.

And now she is coming twelve, and at big school, and they are going to visit the family because the adults have to talk about the summer, and about Granda.

Carrie is sick in the car. Her mam puts her in the front seat, but she is still sick and they have to stop three times. Not just nausea, but actual vomiting into the damp grass at the side of the road. Her da asks if she has been eating crisps. He disapproves of crisps. Her mam says it's a good job they weren't on the motorway and asks if she can't control it? Has she no will power? Granda has willpower. He put the cork in the bottle, didn't he?

Carrie thinks about the last time she was in the pigeon loft, about the laughter, about Granda hurting her arm, about the damp patch. She cannot tell anyone or say anything because there is nothing to tell. Nothing happened. She has no words to describe the atmosphere that was heavy with menace and fear and foreboding. How can you talk about what happened only in your imagination?

She is still heavy and her mam has given her a book about girls growing up, in case she starts early. It is written by Sister Marion. She couches things in the language of her mam's generation, with its vague intimations of dark thoughts, inappropriate feelings. It advises prayer as a remedy. Or the distraction of writing a letter or knitting a scarf. Carrie just says she already knew most of it and her mam nods. Nowhere does it mention standing apart from your imprisoned body and becoming a passive and objective observer while you are somewhere else, and free, in your mind. Or counting. Anything. Just counting.

Maybe she will be too grown-up now to go to the pigeons. But she doubts if she is old enough to sit in on the family discussions. Maybe she can just be left in peace to read. She could sit in the shed if Craig didn't keep it locked all the time. Sharon keeps her room locked, too. So many locks and bolts. The drinks cabinet is always open. You can help yourself to whatever you want. Craig has shown her.

Chapter 7

The Past

THE MINUTE THEY ARRIVE AT THE DOOR SHE knows there is no reprieve. Auntie Vee is tight-lipped. In the kitchen, Sharon and Craig are sitting smoking, an opened bottle of Bacardi between them. The pigeon trophy is on top of the kitchen cabinet. A pile of bills has been stuffed underneath it. It needs dusting. It's still Lent, not that any of them observe it. Her da accepts a bottle of beer. Her mam has a Coke. Auntie Vee says Carrie can have some when she's been down to see Granda at the pigeons. Granda does not sit in a room where there is drinking. Maybe that's why the rest of them drink so much. He knows they are talking about him. What's to be done about him? He has no choice. The tenancy is in Vee's name. She could put him in a home if she wanted.

Two flocks of pigeons have been bred since Carrie was last at the loft. Her granda is at the door, smoking. He looks her up and down, saying nothing. He throws the butt to the path and grinds it with his foot.

'You came. Youse are back.'

He laughed, that chilly laugh, and time reels backwards.

'And I'm going on my holidays with you. Boysaboysaboys.'

Carrie knows nothing of this and her face tells him so.

'That's what they're on about. In there.' He jabs a bony finger in the direction of the house. 'She wants rid of me for a while.'

'Is Auntie Vee poor?' Carrie has no idea why she has asked this. She just blurted it out. Like she has blurted out the F-word at home when she has come back from other visits. It is not used in their house. Mam glares at Da and tells Carrie not to use that word again.

'I give her plenty.'

Granda reaches for the pack of cigarettes in his cardigan pocket, then changes his mind.

'Come in.' A command, not an invitation.

Carrie follows him into the dusty darkness. 'Which one won the trophy?'

Granda opens a cage on the top left-hand side of the loft and takes her out. He holds the bird reverentially. 'She'll win again. She has three races now. But the first was the big one.'

'She's lovely.' In fact, they all look much the same to Carrie.

'We're breeding off her the year. Good strong chicks.

We had a runt or two the last time.'

Carrie knew what happened to the weaklings. The vulnerable. The cock pigeon preyed on them. When they were learning to fly. If a fragile chick fell to the ground, the cock would attack it as it was lying defenceless. He might attempt to copulate with it. He might kill it. His own chick. But this is nature's way.

Yes, this is nature.

'You're getting to be a big girl. Plenty of flesh on you.'

Carrie squirms.

'You're getting real woman now.'

His eyes, up and down her body, burning into her.

'Not like that skinny bitch indoors. With the lock and bolt on her bedroom door.'

Sharon? Or Vee?

'Your mam and da sleep in the one bed?'

Carrie nods. It is the normal thing, in her house. One night, years ago, they had stayed overnight because there had been too much drink and Da couldn't drive home. Auntie Vee had tried to organise the sleeping arrangements. Her da had said the sofa would do fine. Vee wanted her mam and her to share her bed, and put Alex in with Craig, then Da could have Alex's wee bed in the boxroom. From somewhere she had found the courage to say no.

'Just no. Plain and simple.' Auntie Vee had looked like she wanted to slap her. Hard. But she daren't, not with Mam and Da there. In the end, Mam got her way and all three of them crowded into Alex's bed, her squashed into the wall, then Mam in the middle, and Da clinging on to the outside edge.

Sometimes she wondered if it really was so normal. Auntie Vee and Uncle Ron didn't share a bed. They had twin beds and Vee wanted the room to herself. She was saving up for bunks for the boxroom. Then Ron and Alex could sleep there and Sharon would sleep with her furry animals, the same as always. Carrie reckoned Alex would have to take the top bunk. Uncle Ron was too stiff to shimmy up the ladder. But he would do what Vee told him. He always did.

Granda grips her shoulder. Hard.

'I said your ma and da sleep in the same bed?'

Carrie nods.

'Proper fucking order. But there's no talking to that woman.'

Vee? Or Sharon? Are they interchangeable?

'Do you mind how to hold them?'

Carrie nods assent. Granda beckons her further into the loft, opens a cage on the right and puts a young male in her cupped hands. It is tiny. Trembling. He stands close behind her.

'That's a young male. You can't sex them for the first few days. But that's a male. A fine young cock. Your pigeon is the only bird that feeds her young. From the mouth.'

His arms form a cage round her and the bird. 'That's good.'

He strokes her cupped hands.

She shivers involuntarily. 'Your hands are cold.' It is only partly a lie.

'The mother pigeon regurgitates her milk and feeds it to her baby.' He has told her this often. 'She puts her beak right over its wee beak to force it down. That's all it takes for six days. Mother's milk. Swallowed. And regurgitated. The same milk. No other bird does that. From her own mouth.'

This was nature. Natural. So why did it make her flesh creep?

His breathing is heavier, more laboured. He doesn't speak. Carrie clutches the pigeon and tries to think of something to say to break the silence, the tension. Anything.

'I'm at secondary school now. Since September.'

'Still at the books. Like your da.'

His hands close round the soft globes of skin that are developing of their own accord into two plump, floppy pouches streaked with fine red lines. Stretch marks. The nipples are turned in. Inverted. Invisible. Girls write to problem pages to find out if this is a sign of cancer or some other terrible disease. It isn't. It's nature. Marie Spencer at school rubs hers with an ice cube to make them stand out. But then, she is a tart. Carrie's body frightens her. It was out of control. There are fine hairs in her armpits and around her private parts. She is aware of damp patches on her school shirt. Other girls carry deodorant sprays in their PE bags and apply them liberally after gym. Their mothers buy them for them, or they get them with their pocket money when they go up the town on Saturday. Everybody goes up the town on Saturdays, to meet boys and try on the latest fashions, go to the pictures, eat chips and ice-cream sundaes. Especially to meet boys. Carrie has pocket money, always, but she never gets to go up the town. They go visiting on Saturdays. And when she has broached the subject, her mam said she doesn't hold with deodorant. She never uses it herself; she doesn't need it.

Carrie worries about being smelly. She worries about needing a bra. There are so many worries to keep her awake at night. She worries about her puppy fat. The rolls of flaccid, pasty flesh with the texture of soda-bread dough. She worries about people laughing at her. As well as the stomach pains, she has started to come out in an itchy rash as she lies sleepless in the dark, fearful and alone. It is getting harder to escape into her head. Think of chemist's shops. Think of magazine pictures of deodorants. Think of the house you will live in when you grow up, with a fitted kitchen with Formica doors and a lemon bathroom and hot and cold running water and a three-channel TV from Radio Rentals. And a white bedroom with dark blue walls. And a lock.

Granda's hands are kneading her breasts, and she squeals as he forces his thumbnail into the place where her nipple should be. It is sore. Very sore. His breathing is laboured. His voice is thick when he speaks.

'You're getting real woman now. Do the boys be looking at you?'

'I'm not allowed a boyfriend until I leave home to go to university.'

This amuses him.

'That's your da, all right. But that doesn't stop you, does it? Tell me about your wee boys.'

'There aren't any.'

'Liar. Are they horny wee bastards? Do they feel your titties like this?'

'I don't go with boys. I'm not twelve yet.'

He ignores her.

'Do they drop the hand here?' He forces one hand between her thighs.

She clamps her legs together to try to stop him moving it.

He laughs. But his hand stays there.

'I bet they do. I'd give them a good hiding if I caught them at it. Many's the hiding I gave your da. And Vee, when I caught the boys at her. Big and all as she was, I tore the knickers off her and gave her it hot and heavy on the bare arse with a walking stick. That put manners on her. She'd be crying in the bed afterwards,' he goes on. 'And when I got back from the pub I'd go up and rub cream on it for her and we'd make up. We'd be great again. Girls have to learn they lead boys astray. You drive us mad. Youse are all the same. Youse are bad bitches.'

His speech is breaking up. He is gasping for breath. For a dreadful moment, Carrie thinks he is having a heart attack. Then she knows.

'Cock teasers. Bad bitches.'

She freezes, still clutching the bird to her. She is holding it too tight. Its fragile heart is pounding. She hopes she is not hurting it. She tries to walk into a better place, round and round her grown-up house, wiping the Formica doors of the kitchen units, filling the big primrose yellow bath, rose-scented bubbles foaming under the scalding taps.

Her granda shudders and emits one loud, guttural groan. Then as suddenly as he had reached for her, he pushes her away. She thrusts the bird at him and runs towards the house. His laughter follows her. It will haunt her.

Inside the kitchen, Vee tells her to get herself a Coke from the fridge and go and sit on the step and read her book. Or something. They're talking.

Craig follows her out. He is carrying a tumbler of Bacardi and Coke. The tumbler is really a squash glass. Yellow and orange leaves decorate it. A picture of a pineapple.

'Want some?'

Carrie shakes her head.

'Suit yourself. It's good stuff.'

He takes a long swallow then hands her the glass. 'Keep it for me. Drink it if you want. I'm away down to the old boy. He's teaching me how to look after the pigeons when he's on holidays with you. It's all arranged.'

That night Carrie finds a new place to go to in her head. She does not know how it came to be there, but in this place she is counting the beams and the planks and the joists of the pigeon loft, up and down, one by one, then she starts to smash them with an axe, until all that is left is a big pile of wood. Exhausted, covered in sweat, she breaks into Craig's shed and gets the can of petrol he keeps for his motorbike. And a lighter. He keeps lighters everywhere. She lifts the top copy of *Weekend* magazine from the pile in the corner. Slowly, carefully, she pours the petrol over the pyre. Then she tears off the magazine cover, sparks the lighter and throws the flaming page at the woodpile, running away with her hands shielding her face as the flames roar upwards.

Her heart pounds in her chest.

Her stomach thrills with adrenaline, with excitement.

She watches from the end of the garden as it burns to ashes.

Only afterwards does she wonder where the birds have gone.

CHAPTER 8

The Present

I WALK UP THE STEPS TO THE COURTHOUSE AT twenty past ten the next morning. The court's business rarely starts on time, but I need my routine. I check at the desk and the civilian security officer lets me read a copy of the day's lists. I blend in very easily here. Solicitors, barristers, police officers, social workers, probation, victim-support agencies, defendants and witnesses, prosecution and defence. I buy my paper cup of scalding black coffee and move easily among them, always a little bit apart, exchanging nods of recognition, smiles, pleasantries. I have the sort of open face that invites confidences. I look harmless, maybe. Women engage me in conversations in the toilets, or when they're outside having a smoke. Once, a woman confided in me in the most matter-of-fact, objective voice that if she were convicted on a minor theft charge she would throw herself off the train on the way home. I took the day off the next day; I didn't want to know what happened. I felt irrationally guilty by implication. You do get involved, though, in people's lives.

I get to know the very heart and soul of this court: who's really innocent; who's guilty; who's going down; whose case will collapse; what deals are being done behind closed doors. Though, of course, deals do not exist. I hear the back story from the reporters. I hear the undercurrents, the politics, the bad blood, the feuds. I have become important as an indicator of public opinion, the prevailing mood. No-one asks what I do.

One entire court is set aside for the sex cases. There are so many. That's because the retrospective cases – going back ten, twenty, maybe thirty years – are on the same list as the ones from last year, the year before. Those alleged victims are young. They give their evidence by video link from a little room downstairs. Often it doesn't work. The children in the retrospective cases are parents now. Grandparents, even. But it is the wounded child who comes to court to testify not just to what happened but to the stolen, lost years ever since. Sometimes they regress to speak in the voice of the innocent child they once were. Halting. Vulnerable. Honest, for they have not yet learned to lie.

The pigeon man will not appear today. The judge is still considering the point of law. It must be given due consideration, we are told. But it is Thursday, so there are remands by video link. Nothing much happens, but it's a chance to see the defendants face to face on the screen beside the clerk of the court. Families don't come.

Nor do their accusers. There's no point. If a defendant is granted bail, his accuser is supposed to be told. But it doesn't always work out that way. I've lost count of the number of times I've heard a survivor swear that the first they knew their attacker was free was when they bumped into him in the street. I'm quite knowledgeable about the procedures now. People are starting to ask me for advice, for guidance.

The best bit is when I get to read the transcripts of the police interviews. Or the victims' statements. They have phrases and sentences and sometimes whole paragraphs blocked out. But if you get peace to study them – and you do, so long as the court officials know you're not going to report them, and my reputation is impeccable – you get a real feel for the dark mystery that was their past and colours their present. And their future. It's compulsive. I become part of the story, the anonymous observer, the guardian of cruel secrets, some of which may never be made public. I hold the knowledge within me like the gift it is. I have a right to it.

Today I read how a young babysitter has confessed to inappropriate touching of his young charges. How an eight-year-old girl will not give evidence alongside her sister, as the police say she would not be a credible witness and how this has driven her family apart, one side saying she should be encouraged to forget what happened and move on, the other that she must withstand the rigours of cross-examination and tell her truth. How a favourite uncle has invited his nephew's silence with cartoon videos and chocolate bars and secured it with threats of retribution, disgrace, or, worst of all, disbelief.

No-one will believe you.

No-one will want to believe you.

No-one will choose to believe you.

You keep your secrets. Your dirty, cancerous secrets. Your truth.

I have had enough for one day. The past is rising and threatens to engulf and develop the present. It happens less now, much less, except in dreams. This is my compulsion, but it is time to step out, into the sun.

CHAPTER 9

The Past

THE CHICKS ARE FLYING THE NEXT TIME Carrie visits the pigeon shed.

It's a big event in the pigeon calendar. The club's best racing birds have been despatched in their wicker hampers the day before and at two fifteen today they will be released, near the port of Cherbourg, to wing their way back. More little birds braving the grey skies over the English Channel and the Irish Sea, battling their unerring way home through southwesterly winds and intermittent spring showers. Carrying on their frail legs not urgent messages from the Western Front but the rings that will clock in their flight time and the heavy burden of the off-course betting on their backs. These are champion birds; some will vanish, blown out of the sky and drowned, dead from exposure, easy prey to predators. Craig says that the birds are all insured and if one of his hopefuls comes back so slowly as to make a mockery of him, he'll wring its neck and claim on the insurance.

A crowd is gathering while Granda and Craig keep their vigil. Rumours are traded. Spies are sent out from the loft to suss out the rumours that rival birds have been clocked in already. In the kitchen, Auntie Vee gets out the two basketwork trays that Granda made at the day centre before he told them where to stick their occupational therapy. They have yellow and blue plastic beads threaded into the basketwork edges. One has a laminated base depicting red roses, the other has a fruit bowl. The red roses tray is now covered with heaps of little triangles of ham sandwiches and individually wrapped chocolate wafer biscuits and teacakes. The tray with the fruit motif has bottles of stout and a gentleman's bottle of whiskey, a jug of water and glasses. Later, the women will make tea and bring a mug to Granda, who will not come into the kitchen to join the men toasting success or drowning their sorrows. For Granda, much to everyone's continuing amazement, it seems, has put the cork in the bottle and kept it there. Now he has also stopped betting. There are no more messages to the bookies with names for the ITV Seven. In the army, her da has told her, there were men like Granda who would have bet on two flies crawling up a wall. No more. It elicits grudging respect from the most dubious and hostile of corners, including her mam, but it is an accepted fact that Granda's only vice now is his fags. Sixty a day, untipped. And his pigeons. Soon, though, they will be Craig's pigeons, the whole flock, not just three or four. It is a rite of passage.

Granda likes Craig. He hates Auntie Vee and Uncle Ron and Sharon and Alex and her mam and he tolerates her da. And the brown envelopes keep changing hands.

They stand round, smoking. Carrie is sent up to the house for Granda's tea. He tells her to tell Vee not to be sending him down anything to eat because he won't eat it. She is sent back with his mug of strong black tea with three sugars and two rounds of bread and margarine, which he throws into the hedge. For the birds. Craig snatches the plate from him before it can go the same way. Carrie has also been sent back with the instructions that the drinks are poured and Craig is to come up to the kitchen. She is to keep watch with Granda.

Her stomach is churning and her heart pounds with the sense of the inevitable but she has no way of stopping what she knows is about to happen.

'Come here, girl.'

She walks into the dusty gloom of the shed. Granda pushes shut the door. The men will stay in the kitchen for a second or third drink, long enough for the pools results to come on the telly. It is her duty to keep him company, away from the drink, the temptation.

This afternoon, Carrie has planned to go to Granada Studios and win a heat of *Opportunity Knocks*, though she isn't sure what she will do in front of the cameras. Singing is easiest, but she can't sing, and it helps if you are young and have big eyes and a sad story to tell. Like maybe your mother has died. But no-one wants to know her sad story. There are no mitigating circumstances or vote-catching pathos in the death of hope.

It is like the last time, and the time before, she thinks, but she is not certain, as she has stepped outside her body again and is enjoying her dream too much to pay much attention to what's going on with her body. She knows her cotton dress will reek of stale smoke and pigeon feed, the nauseating smell of curdled milk and the acrid fumes of stale urine. So will her hair. Carrie wishes they had a proper bathroom where she could have a bath every night to wash away the day. She will add that to one of her dreams, she decides, the one with the Formica kitchen units and the three-channel TV and the hostess trolley and her own lock on the door.

Afterwards, she is aware of someone looking at her. From the corner of her eye she sees the door to the loft has opened a few inches and Craig is standing there, sipping from a bottle of beer. And watching. How much has he seen?

Afterwards, Carrie sees Craig palming her granda a brown envelope. Carrie wonders if maybe Granda hasn't stopped gambling after all.

The first of his flock makes it home just after six.

It has not won but it may get a placement. Granda curses, long, venomous curses, and kicks the side of the loft with his boot.

Craig smiles at her and offers her a beer. He is unusually talkative. He is in company. He introduces a few of his friends, who look a bit older than him and whose names she instantly forgets, but not the way they look her up and down. They are Pigeon Men, too, he says, and laughs.

That night, Mam and Da tell her that Granda is coming for two weeks at Easter, as an experiment. Vee needs a break; her nerves are shattered. Carrie lies awake in her single bed, kneading the loose rolls of blighted skin on her inner thighs, squeezing at her flaming boils until they burst open, wiping up the pus on a tissue and examining it, comforted by the dark, dull throbbing it leaves, the hard lumps embedded deep into the skin. There are no locks in their house. There never have been. She feels her stomach burn with acid and scratches the thin skin of her upper arms until the pale white itchy spots break through, surrounded by great reddish-pink blotches. If her granda can get his thing hard, she knows he will put it inside her. He has told her so. When he can't, he becomes frustrated and lashes out. There are dark bruises coming up on the inside of her forearm and more on her hips. Her body is a disaster area. She remembers as if from another life that he had unbuckled the belt from his trousers and she had almost wet herself thinking he was going to beat her with it. Instead he had wrapped it round her throat and pulled her into him. She had been gasping for breath, dizzy, but he had kept laughing, holding the leather noose taut round her neck, jerking on the slip knot to shake her in and out. It had rubbed a raw patch on her neck. Carrie was terrified her parents would think it was a love bite. Some of the girls come to school with them rising like badges of honour out of their white nylon shirt collars. You are supposed to put toothpaste on them to make them fade. Or to say you have a sore throat, wear a polo neck and hand in a forged excuse note. Carrie thinks they are ugly, especially the ones where the flesh has bruised and discoloured into concentric rings – grey, purple, mauve, red, pink. Like war wounds. But they mean you are loved. Or so some of the girls say.

Her mother says Carrie got herself worked up over nothing, just like Vee. She is like a lot of the women on her father's side of the family, her mother thinks. Too highly strung. And she needs to grow up and catch herself on.

CHAPTER 10

The Past

GRANDA COMES FOR THREE WEEKS. NOT TWO. The night before they go to collect him, Carrie is so wound up she cannot eat her dinner. Her da shouts at her and she bursts into tears, wiping her face, for whatever reason, on the tablecloth. She apologises immediately, says she doesn't know what came over her. Her da walks out of the room, puzzled. Carrie has never been a day's bother. Good at her books, keeps the head down. She will go on to study medicine, law or be a bilingual secretary in Brussels, which is the future and where she will get great money and never need to settle down and have a husband and children unless she really, really wants to. Carrie doesn't want to be a doctor or a lawyer or a bilingual secretary and live in Brussels and have great money. She wants to live in a house with a fitted kitchen with Formica doors and a primrose yellow bathroom with a lock and a fluffy white bedroom and a three-channel TV and a baby and a cat. But no-one has ever asked her what she wants. She does her homework and passes her exams and eats her dinners and reads her books and has to believe that when she has done all these things enough times to please people, she will be free of it. Forever.

Her mam takes her upstairs and hugs her and tries to find out what's really wrong. She asks Carrie is she checking for stains on her knickers and Carrie replies that she is and her mam says it's strange because she went early and you'd think Carrie would go early, too, as she is big. Big means fat.

Carrie seizes her chance and tells her mam she thinks she needs a bra. One of her friends has told her it's easy – just ask her mam to take her up to the department store in town early one Saturday, before they go to Granda's, and get her fitted for one of the bras that everybody in the class seems to have, the floral or the check, the pinks and reds or the blues. They're not dear, the friend says, and surely her mam must expect it. Carrie wishes so much it was easy. In the end, her mam says 'we'll see' and to Carrie's amazement a few weeks later she produces one ordered by post from a catalogue that is an old woman's design and will show through her school shirt and doesn't fit her anyway. Her da asks her mam if it will do. And when she says no, he looks frustrated and disgusted, this complex world of adolescence and womanhood both a burden and a mystery. Her mam tells her some of the girls at school are silly wanting bras and the next thing they'll be wanting to go after boys and that'll be the end of them and their studies and they'll never get to university and they'll end up with boys from around home and it'll all be dumped on their family's doorstep.

Carrie knows that there will be plenty of time for boys when she leaves home and she is not to go about with anyone from home, so there will be no talk about her and nothing brought back to the doorstep.

Her sister, Helen, must have obeyed to a T, because she had met a man from England in her first week at university and never came home again. She has a big job. She should have been a doctor but she is a senior university lecturer, which is nearly as good. She earns good money. She has no children. Her graduation photos are on the wall – MSc. Ph.D. Success. Her mam is kind tonight, and says she will make her something new to wear, even though Carrie is fat and all she can wear is smocks. Her mam buys paper patterns in teenage sizes then adds on about four inches to each piece. Her da favours bright colours. Cheerful.

Carrie hates wearing them. She wishes she could blend into the background and disappear. She is also old enough to drink at home now, they agree, and she gets her sherry before Sunday dinner, her hot whiskey on a Saturday night, her glass of table wine. Visitors bring her Babycham. Carrie likes the way it makes her feel. It is better than stories to make your head go away to where nobody can touch you. Her mam and da tell her it is important to drink at home because it is better value for money and more private and nobody can talk about you. You do not buy your alcohol near home for the same reason. Like bras and deodorants and condoms, it comes from far away. It is good for young people to learn to drink like they do on the continent, she is told, so they do not go mad on it when they leave home. By the time she leaves home, Carrie will be able to drink her friends under the table and will be bemused by the girls who get all silly and giggly after three Cinzano Bianco.

But that is far away and Granda will be there when she gets back from school. He will be in what was Helen's room. The door to that room can actually be shut, though with difficulty, for the wood of the door has swollen and warped. It has creeping ivy on the wallpaper.

Granda does not unpack the suitcase that Auntie Vee has sent with him. During the day, he paces up and down the street outside, smoking, and sends youngsters to the shop for his cigarettes. Indoors, he sits in the front room and smokes and reads cowboy books or watches the TV. He complains that they can only get BBC. Her mam tells him the mountains get in the way of good reception and they only have it because of Carrie; if it were left up to her, it would never be on. In the evenings, Carrie dreads the time when her mam and da are having their nightcap in the kitchen, or doing the crossword, or reading, and talking. It is worst when she hears the front door open and she knows they are going out to stroll through the fresh spring evening, hand in hand, happy. It takes an hour to walk the round route. She watches the clock, willing it on. She goes to the toilet, far too often. She makes coffee. And she sits in the front room with Granda. They watch TV and read. He likes sport and the sitcoms. The news makes him angry. Carrie sits rigid, her eyes on the door, waiting for her granda to move, to say something. His eyes look her up and down, knowingly, and he laughs that bitter laugh. He tells her her mam and da should enjoy the drink while they can. Still he makes no move. It is as if nothing has ever happened between them, yet the tension is everywhere, charging the atmosphere. His words have hidden meanings. Rich with sexual innuendo, deprecating remarks about women. Her face burns with embarrassment, yet she knows there is no shame; she has done nothing.

She sees him with the paperback Western open on his lap, watching the TV, feeling his crotch. She knows if he can get it to harden he will attack her with it. And her worst fears will be vindicated. She is right. She has to be right. It does not happen to everybody. She should not brush it aside and put it all behind her. These are not the dark thoughts mentioned in Sister Marion's booklet. If prayer could have stopped her granda, it would have done so long ago. She cannot be that bad a person. Why her? Why not Helen? But they did not go to Auntie Vee's when her sister was young. There is no point in trying to write to Helen for help. She wouldn't write back. There is no-one else she can talk to, even if she could find the words. Her mam has not told her about sex, apart from the Sister Marion booklet. So how can

Carrie tell her what she thinks – she knows – is happening to her? Would it be like the bra and the deodorant episodes? Voiced then ignored?

When Granda goes home, her da says he was a grumpy old bastard but nowhere near as bad as Vee had made out. Carrie is beyond the fear of sleeping. Her stomach is convulsed in pain. Her itchy rash is worse. She lies awake at night, sweating and shaking. Her mam takes her to the doctor, who gives her an injection that makes her sleep for twenty-four hours. He calls the next day as she lies dozing. She hears the good and gentle doctor asking about stress, academic pressure, weight issues. He gives her tablets but says a girl her age, not yet thirteen, should not really be on them. The tablets are small and blue and they conjure up the escape dreams for Carrie. She swallows them and the world goes on around her but without her – she is observing it from a warm, slow, medicated cocoon. She is a passive spectator in her own life.

She knows the doctor will not be welcomed into their home again. She dreads the conversation where her parents will act as if she is not there and the doctor's questions were somehow her fault.

'I think he was too ready to blame us for putting too much pressure on her. If that school would do what they're there for … but they're far too easy going.' Her mam's voice sounding irritated.

'You'd wonder who put that notion into his head. It's all this modern stuff about having to blame your problems on your childhood. I don't think we'll be going near that particular surgery for a while, do you?' Her da's head shaking, annoyed.

'Blame the parents. That's what they all say. It's the easy option.' Her mam, she knows, is casting her eyes heavenwards.

People should mind their own business, keep their own secrets. That is the message. Unspoken but understood.

The prescription is repeated, twice, then there are no more pills and the night terrors return.

CHAPTER 11

The Past

SPRING DRAGS INTO SUMMER. GRANDA IS back at Vee's. Carrie's mam says for as long as he hands over his pension money, Vee will hang on in there to inherit whatever there is and anyway, the old boy could have money stashed away, you would never know. Carrie does well in her exams. Very well. She will be allowed to skip another year and go straight into the first year of her O Levels provided she works over the summer holidays. She has a long reading list to order from the mobile library and she orders not just a selection but every possible text on the English syllabus. She works through the Maths and Biology and the Geography and History texts. Only the French perplexes her. She learns the vocabulary by heart but is unsure about the pronunciation. Her parents insist on helping her, but she knows the school books they have unearthed are outdated and their grasp of phonetics is embarrassing, their pronunciation a parody of the real thing. She says nothing. There is no point. Instead, she gets them to set her memory tests. They demand a hundred per cent. They usually get it. Carrie is happy that she is making them happy. There is nothing else to do over the long summer holiday with her classmates miles away. And they will not be her classmates when she goes back in the autumn. Her da dreams of a scholarship to Oxford or Cambridge. He suggests she should learn an extra language at home to give herself a head start. He sends for some tapes from the BBC but they can't get them to play on their antiquated tape machine and he spends hours winding and rewinding them with a pencil when they stick. Eventually, the machine shreds them.

She persuades her mam to let her da go on his own to visit the family, as she wants to get on with her work. She knows Mam hates them. Mam agrees. It's good, just the two of them, reading and writing and listening to the radio, in the same room. Late that night, while she reads and absently watches the TV, the sound turned down, she hears him in the kitchen, telling her mam that Vee had a go at him about Carrie being strange. Her granda had asked for her. He said he and Craig could do with a hand with the pigeons. It was a joke, of course, but it's great the way they had taken to Carrie. He had sent her a pound note. Carrie folded it up in tiny squares and put it in her savings purse.

At night, she lies, sleepless, going up and down the length of her body, recording the imperfections, mortifying the flesh. The flushed cheeks. The open pores. The grey shadows under her eyes. The acne. The whiteheads on her upper arms that turn red when she squeezes them till the white core pops out. More whiteheads on her nipples. Boils under her drooping breasts, around her navel, her bottom, her inner thighs, even her vulva. Some filled with yellow pus; some hard red and throbbing under the skin which bleed fresh blood; some with a core that will pop; some weeping clear fluid.

Some of her nails have been torn off, fingers and toes, and the skin beside her fingernails has been chewed and pulled away. There is an actual hole in the surface of one of her nails, maybe two. The pain helps. It comforts, it distracts, it soothes. It is her secret. Another dirty secret. But this one is hers. She controls it. She hides it. Every night, she ends her ritual of self-disgust by pulling strips of skin off the soles of her feet. The soles are dark red and raw in places. The blood congeals by the morning. And as she lies, sleepless, the rash appears, raised white lumps on her arms and legs that itch. Her stomach burns with acid and she tries different positions in the bed to ease the pain. She loathes herself. She despises the reflection in the mirror. She sees no way out. Years later, she will learn about self-harm. She will hear her mother's judgement that if these things weren't talked about and written about, nobody would get the idea of trying them. It's attention seeking. She never tells.

Reluctantly, her mam takes her back to the doctor's and it is a visiting locum, a lovely woman who asks to see Carrie on her own. Her mam disapproves but has no choice. The doctor asks her gently about her weight. Carrie is amazed to find the doctor thinks she is eating behind her parents' back. Does she not know that is impossible, that Carrie never goes anywhere to buy food? That Carrie dreams of looking normal? Her mam is brought back in and the doctor remains gentle, but firm. Carrie, she says, will miss out on so much. In her teenage years. Friendships. Boys. Hobbies. Social life. Her mam says something about there being plenty of time for that when she leaves home to go to university. Her mam says they have been trying to diet, which is a total lie. The doctor gives her a calorie sheet. She expresses grave reservations about the tablets Carrie has been on but she renews the prescription. Half the women in the estate are on them, it seems, but they are not twelve years old.

Her mam is tight-lipped going home. Later it will be discussed, over a drink, with her da. They will bond in mutual disapproval of the interfering trendies who have been allowed to qualify as doctors. Carrie's sister should have been one. It was all the fault of the school. Too easy going.

By the end of the week her mam has thrown out the calorie chart, saying it cannot possibly be accurate and doesn't account for things like what happens to all the ingredients you put into a cake tin. Maybe if you divided the total by ten that would be about right. Her da says home-made food is good for you and it's shop-bought buns and crisps that make you fat. Her da hates crisps. They are a symbol of idle motherhood and families poor by their own hand. It is a sin to waste food and we all need something to fall back on in case we get an illness.

Skinny is like nylon underwear and soap operas on TV and smoking and hanging about with boys and slot machines and funfairs and long hair (either sex) and women who go to the shops bare legged and a dozen and one other things that Carrie knows she will find out are unacceptable. But she has very little idea of how the list is comprised.

If she makes even the most tentative approaches to the subject of older men touching up girls, she knows it is on the list of things you should get over because they happen to everyone and those who don't get over it are on the same list as wives who dislike sex, women who refuse to have a second child because of the pain of childbirth and women who are bad with their nerves.

Carrie wonders why they imagine she has been prescribed the medication she is on.

No-one talks about it.

No-one talks about any of it.

Back at school, her classmates are kind, but distant. They do not bully. They do not tease. They may even pity her. Her mam sees one or two of them in the street, with boys. They are ridiculed in front of Carrie. Her parents know what will happen to them. They smile in collusion. Carrie is told not to speak to such stupid girls. Carrie says nothing. She has retreated into herself. It's getting harder to get back into her body from the place where she watches her life happening as if to someone else.

They go to see Granda once a fortnight. He is getting frail. His chest is weak from years of smoking. He blames the Western Front. Craig does more and more with the pigeons. More and more, Granda lies in his bed in the attic rather than out in the pigeon shed and Carrie gets sent up to him with tea and to keep him company because he has asked for her. She sits on the floor by the door and when she takes over the tea he grabs and pulls at her, clamping his mouth over hers, slobbering over her, forcing his tongue between her lips, grabbing her crotch. And now because she is getting 'real woman', he thrusts a bony finger inside her and she cries out when his horny nail scrapes her skin. He pulls and kneads at her breasts and for a supposedly frail man his grip is surprisingly strong. She pulls away and sits at the door. He starts to talk about school, about Craig, as if nothing has happened. Then he laughs. As he always does. That bitter, mocking laugh of secret power. As soon as the tea is drunk, she escapes downstairs and promises to go back, but she won't. Auntie Vee gives her a bottle of beer and a glass of whiskey to take down to the pigeon loft for Craig. It is no longer an alcohol-free zone. Auntie Vee rues the day she ever let Craig get interested in the pigeons, because otherwise she could get rid of them when Granda dies.

Craig has been drinking from early on. Carrie realises he is quite drunk. He keeps smiling at her, and laughing, not in a bitter way like Granda, not mocking, but still in a way that makes her feel vulnerable. Dirty. His eyes linger on her breasts, the hem of her skirt. As she reaches over the bottle and glass, he tells her her skirt is too short. He says she is getting real grown-up. The perfect age, her granda calls it. The perfect age. His move is swift and sudden as he pulls her to him and forces his mouth over hers. The same way her granda did. 'My wee cousin,' he whispers, as he puts his hand up her skirt and rubs the crotch of her knickers. He feels it is wet and he laughs, as if pleased with himself. She is aware of his erection pushing against her and hears him grunting that this, this is what the old boy wanted but he's past it, he can't get it up any more, he's fucked, as he pushes her to the ground and holding her wrists with one hand he pulls aside her knickers with the other. With terrifying clarity, Carrie realises what he is going to do. In her mind she kicks and screams but in reality she lies frozen, silent. The next thing she remembers, he is calling her frigid, a prick tease, she is too tight. He kicks her in the stomach then turns his back to her and jacks himself off over the meal bags.

'Next time it'll be in your mouth, bitch. That'll sort you out.' His eyes are cold, but the rage has gone.

'And you'd better get yourself loosened up. I have a few boys wanting to meet you. I'll have them up the next day. We'll get a wee drink into you first. A wee Bacardi. You like your Bacardi, don't you, Carrie? We'll get you sorted.'

He hands her two empty beer bottles. She sees he has his own half-bottle of whiskey in the loft. 'Take these to Vee.'

Carrie stumbles out the door and runs to the house. She leaves the bottles on the kitchen table and rushes straight out to the bathroom where she bolts the door and scrubs and scrubs at herself with cold water, rubbing her skin raw with a towel. She is aware of Vee saying something about manners but she doesn't care.

In the car on the way home she is silent. She chooses not to be there. She has outgrown the dream of the Formica kitchen units and the primrose bathroom suite and the fluffy white bedroom. She is almost thirteen now and her dreams are of a tiny flat in a big city, perhaps Dublin, perhaps London, that is hers and hers alone. She cleans and polishes and scrubs it in her mind, until it is perfect.

On bad days she finds herself fantasising about dismantling the loft, chopping up the wooden planks and making a pyre of them. Pouring petrol on them, watching them burn, the purification of fire. These dreams frighten her. They are not good dreams to be having when you are not yet thirteen. She prefers the anxiety dreams about failing her exams and going into an exam without having enough revision done. At least she can work harder. Then it won't happen.

Nothing can stop what is happening to her.

CHAPTER 12

The Past

IT HAPPENS IN NOVEMBER. THE STAIN ON HER knickers is brownish and she hopes against hope that it is poo and not her period. She doesn't feel any different. The spots, the sweating, have been there for a year or more. She has no pains. She checks and checks all day, in and out of the toilet until by tea time there is no mistaking the reddish brown for what it is. She sniffs at the stain. It smells stale and yet strangely compulsive. She tells her mam. Her mam tells her da and she is embarrassed. Her mam says it is important not to be, these things happen to us all, and thank God there isn't ignorance like there used to be when that poor wee girl thought she had cancer and killed herself and that's what started the Samaritans. It is nothing to be ashamed of and Mam expected it ages ago. According to Sister Marion, her mam would have everything ready for her, maybe even tucked away in her own dressing-table drawer, so she could see to herself. But they have to get the car and drive to the town and a bad time because the shops will be closing and they go into the chemist who knows them and it is the same embarrassment over again as her mam explains that no, she doesn't want her usual, and she and the chemist mutter to each other about whether Carrie could use tampons yet and how handy they are. They decide not and the chemist produces a cardboard box hiding a ghastly device made of rubber and white tape and press fasteners to wear under her pants and a dozen towels in pink plastic wrapping with a motif of a flying bird. Carrie thinks it may be a dove, though she cannot imagine what it is meant to symbolise. She knows the girls at school do not wear these, that there are special nylon knickers with a clip in them to hold a much smaller towel in place, with bright floral packaging and you can wear your own knickers over them if you are afraid of what they always refer to as 'embarrassing leaks'. She knows they are advertised in the teenage magazines but they do not order them from the paper shop, as they are all about boyfriends. The contraption looks so antiquated and cumbersome that she remembers the brand name and quotes it hopefully to the chemist who says she has heard of them and will try and get them for next month but that there is no real demand round here. Maybe in the town.

Next month.

That night, although the pain has not yet started, Carrie sobs at the thought of the next few months – months of cramps and unmistakable smell and stale underwear ahead of her. Her mother comes into her room and tells her she has always been so good about things and not to be so silly, to think about something else. Carrie has been doing this for years, but tonight the dream will not come when it is bidden.

She does not need Sister Marion. She knows full well what this means and if her granda or, more likely, Craig comes at her now she could get pregnant.

The next weekend when they go to Granda's, her mam tells them and Auntie Vee advises her to drink brandy and port for the pains and lie down with a hot-water bottle, for it is just another of life's sorrows and tribulations that women must face.

Her granda is still in bed a lot. Vee thinks he has taken a slight stroke, but he won't hear of a doctor and her da says they must get one and Vee tells him he can try, the man is a stubborn old bastard and always has been.

Vee sends her to the loft with a big bottle of whiskey, as Craig has friends round. He treats it as a wee den. They play cards and listen to the radio. He stays around home more, now, Vee says. Less of the disappearing act. Carrie wants to tell her that Craig has his own bottle down in the loft but realises that it is probably long finished. Maybe he keeps more bottles locked in his shed. With his magazines and his petrol can and his leathers and, although Carrie does not know it, a handgun that he is keeping for a friend of a friend.

She has no choice. Perhaps she can get in and out quickly. But even as she says it to herself, she knows it is a lie. Some intangible magnetic force draws her towards the shed. She has never felt more powerless. Time to disappear into her head.

There are three of them in the loft, playing five-card brag. They are well drunk. Loud. Good humoured as Craig makes the introductions of the friends, the lads who wanted to meet her. They splash out the whiskey from the new bottle, raise a mug to her mouth, vacate a stool for her, offer to deal her in. Carrie protests that she doesn't know how to play, she doesn't want a drink, and suddenly the raucous laughter turns menacing and the door is kicked shut and locked and the radio is turned up to drown out her screams and it will be more than twenty years before Carrie remembers everything that happened. Everything they did to her.

Darkness has fallen and the lads have long since gone when her da finds her, huddled up, silent, in the loft. He kicks the empty whiskey bottle and swears about them for getting her drunk, about taking things too far. He gets Carrie to her feet and she stumbles out the door and vomits her guts onto the grass. She is shaking. Cold. Very cold. Between her legs aches, sore and raw, her back passage aches. She knows when she looks at her knickers there will be blood. Auntie Vee and her mam and Sharon come to the back door and her mam runs to her, making wild threats to Vee, who is muttering about the Linley lad being a bad lot and his friend no better and she has warned Craig about hanging around with them. But Craig has told her they are pigeon experts and as such command respect. Granda's birds need them.

CHAPTER 13

The Past

CARRIE DOES NOT SPEAK. ALL THE WAY HOME in the car, in the bath, after she has gone to bed. She says nothing. The pain is there but she feels nothing. She has retreated into her head. Her mam and da come into the room, neither saying anything but talking in unison. Carrie is sorry for being a silly girl about the drink and the boys. She nods. She won't do it again. Vee and Ron will have a word with Craig. She is only thirteen, plenty of time for that later. Maybe she should sit in the room with Granda and not go down to the loft. Granda will be coming here soon, to stay, so that'll break the routine. She nods.

The next morning, her rashes are so bad that her mam keeps her off school. She is off all week. She is given an extra tablet each morning to help her pull herself together. Her mam suggests they should bake, that she should tidy her room, do the ironing, study at home. Carrie agrees. It makes her parents happy and it is irrelevant, unimportant, as she is not there and all these things are being done by someone else who is working her body.

On Saturday, her da wants them to go to the family to sort things out. He is still unhappy. Her mam wants to sort out Craig. Carrie has never been any bother, not till now. And she would need to stop sulking and pull herself together before she goes back to school on Monday. She will have a lot of catching up to do.

Craig is not there. Granda is in bed. Sharon and Alex and Ron and Vee and her parents sit round the kitchen table. Only Vee has a drink in front of her, for her nerves are shattered. It is medicinal, the doctor has advised it, three times a day.

'Away up to your granda,' her da urges her. 'Take a book in case he's sleeping.'

Instead, she tiptoes out the front door that is never opened and pushes it almost shut, ever so quietly. She creeps down the garden to the loft. Craig's bike has gone but the shed is unlocked. He must have gone in a hurry. Carrie slips inside. She lifts a pile of magazines, the can of petrol, a lighter. She carries them over to the loft. She tears out the pages and makes them into little twists and scatters them over the floor. She douses them with petrol. Then she says goodbye to the pigeons. They will love her, these pigeons, for she is giving them their freedom. Better to risk the predator outside than to be locked away from light and air and life and free will. She climbs the ladder and, one by one, moving faster and faster, she opens the cages and the birds fly free. She watches them soar up into the darkening winter sky and disappear from view. She clicks the lighter, two, three times before it sparks and the petrol is ablaze.

She sits on the cement path outside the loft and waits for them to come for her.

Chapter 14

The Past

CARRIE IS DISCHARGED AFTER SIX WEEKS. SHE has been a model patient. Her medication has been increased. She has said little in the hospital, except that she is sorry and she doesn't know what happened. And she realises it's true: she genuinely doesn't know. Her mam and da are pleased with her because she hasn't talked rubbish or washed any dirty linen in public or blamed anything other than her own introspection and overactive imagination for her troubles.

There are follow-up home visits, from the kind GP, to her parents' disappointment, and from the silence of her room Carrie hears them all playing the blame game. The kind GP asks again about exam pressure, speaks of the dangers of ambitious parents, pushing ahead of your contemporaries. Her parents present their united front. The school is not what it was, no ambition, no push, teachers they would be doubtful about, an obsession with weight and appearance, modern thinking, television, magazines, some girls in her year that the school doesn't seem to do anything about. But Carrie has insisted she has not been bullied and it is true; she is, if anything, treated with sympathy. She is an oddity, an outsider. But none of this matters, for she is not going to school on Monday, the GP says. She is going to be educated at home for a while, then eased back into school.

She flies through her lessons. She sits her exams in a room on her own and flies through them, too. She is pleased and surprised to find her uniform is hanging on her. She has no appetite. She refuses food. Her parents apply the third-person treatment.

'She's not having any, Daddy.'

'Well, this pudding is very good. Oh, boy, is it good! Are you sure she won't have a wee taste? Leave her a wee bit. Put it in a wee dish and put a bit of foil over it. Just in case she changes her mind.'

Then her mam: 'When I find out who put this bloody nonsense into her head …'

And her da's repetition of a long-held belief: 'Sure everybody needs a bit to fall back on, in case you're ill.'

The ghost of TB is never named.

Carrie is learning to lie. For herself. And to deceive. She's got a diet book out of the mobile library and hidden it in her room. It is out of date, basic, but it has a calorie chart and she can count up her thousand calories a day. She should lose two pounds a week. She feels the hunger at night, but then she is on sleeping tablets

81

anyway, and going without food gives her a good, light-headed feeling, not unlike drink, which together with her tablets, which she knows are tranquillizers, helps her to stay in her private place most of the time while the books get read and the schoolwork gets done and she watches TV, smiles as her skin shrinks back on her frame. She keeps counting the numbers, memorising them in her head, writing them in the back of her note-pad, starting from a thousand and counting down. She is very good at numbers. Numbers are important. If the numbers are right, then everything else will be right. The numbers are her secret. She is always counting.

She is very helpful around the house and never complains. They never talk about what happened. About the fire. It is treated as an accident. Her parents are baffled. It is better that way. But she does not go visiting.

They ask another doctor about her losing weight and he is delighted. He says Carrie is much healthier now. That doctor will not be back, either. They make her milky drinks, so she has them instead of meals. She chews food and secretes the mush in tissues. If she is really hungry, she puts it back in her mouth, later, and chews it again. But she does not swallow it. She has no young to nourish. She loses contact with the world, biding her time in her chemical incubator, building up her strength until it is time to escape.

When she goes back to school, in sixth form, she is a different person on the outside. Her mam buys her a school skirt from a chain store and it almost fits. It is too big. Her mam is frightened. She insists – *insists!* – she is fitted for bras and her mam voices her incredulity at her smaller size. Even her face looks different. The acne has gone, a blessed side effect of one of the tablets to regulate her periods and stop the occasional, inexplicable bleeding. She tries tampons but finds them too sore. Her mam casts her eyes to heaven and says she hopes she'll grow out of it. Soon. She is still offered a drink with her parents, 'to keep them company', and occasionally she takes one, perhaps a sherry, or a whisky mac, but really she's not bothered. And she counts the calorie numbers. Her parents reassure themselves with comfortable commonplaces. They talk about how much better value it is to buy from an off-licence and drink at home, and how you cannot be careful enough, as some of the drinks they are selling nowadays have hardly any proof at all – four and five per cent wines! Thirty per cent spirits! You have to shop carefully, they agree. She has been told that she can go with as many boys as she wants when she leaves home to go to university but to be careful around a man who doesn't drink. And they should not be from round here where anyone would know them. And she's not to be running home every weekend, she's to get on with it. Helen was allowed home one weekend a term. Carrie remembers that she never came home at all.

Carrie does not go visiting. She offers no reasons but she will give no quarter. Sometimes Mam stays with her; sometimes she is allowed to stay at home on her own to study. She loves this. She plays house, cooks her own tea, watches her own programme, walks about in her dressing gown. Bit by bit, she is seeing a future.

She hears that Craig has been away and come back again. There are reports he has fathered a child to what Vee calls 'some trollop who is after their money, a ring and a roof over her head'. Craig drinks too much. Vee is worried. They blame the popular brand of sweet, blended spirit he has taken to. If he stuck to the beer and whiskey, he would be all right. Her da has paid for the loft but it will not be rebuilt. Granda is not well and Craig comes and goes too much. There are rumours of paramilitary associations, friends who are not good ones. Craig has no job but he always has money.

Carrie is allowed make-up, hair dye, nail polish. She has nails!

She flies through her exams. Little by little, she tells some of her more empathic classmates little details about the restrictions of her home life. Surprisingly, they understand. They reach out to her. She does not mention these friends at home. The friends are seen in public with boys, go to discos, even on holidays, get part-time jobs. Her parents do not know, so they cannot comment. They do not visit the school; they have given up on it as a dead loss.

Carrie does not tell her friends about the Pigeon Men. She has no words to do so.

In the spring of her final year, Granda is taken to hospital with a stroke. It is not his first, because he is a stubborn old bastard who would not seek help, but it is his last and he dies, three weeks later.

Carrie and her mam do not go to the funeral. The day before, Sharon goes berserk in the house and the doctor has to be called to sedate her. She has been rummaging through Granda's room, turning out drawers, emptying the pockets of jackets, rooting about under the bed. Auntie Vee says Sharon was always fond of him and is distraught with grief. She makes a holy show of herself at the funeral.

Granda must have left her money, for Sharon books a week in Tenerife for herself and her girlfriends. She dyes her hair and signs up for tanning and toning sessions. She buys a whole new wardrobe of clothes, including a fun fur, which is much admired, even though it is May.

Her da says you would think her granda might have left Carrie something, as he was fond of her, but if he did, they will never see it, as Sharon has scooped the pool.

When Sharon goes to Tenerife, Alex moves back to live with his mother. She is said to be not too well and no-one will say how long he will be staying. Auntie Vee says he was an inoffensive creature, but thank God he has gone, because he had a way of getting on her nerves, sitting there smoking and sipping his cans and saying nothing. And Craig had never liked him. Uncle Ron takes up fishing. He disappears for entire days with his friends and never comes home with so much as a box of fish fingers. Auntie Vee says he is getting strange, but it's his age and at least she has the house the way she wants it, because, to be honest, he got on her nerves, too. She does not trust quiet men.

Carrie thinks she may be a bit happy now. There is a big library in school and she has done her research on the courses she would like, made her applications during her free periods. Her teachers are pleased and because her parents do not come to the school, they do not know. When they discuss her career, in the third person, she goes into her mental incubator. She has not lied to them, for she has no idea what she has agreed to.

She knows she will get the grades. And she does. She is still very young, she could take another year out to try for Cambridge, but the school advises against it, so there is nothing anyone can do to make her.

The day the results come, she hides in the toilet, not frightened of opening the little self-addressed envelope but wanting to savour the moment, to hold on to it for-ever. A good memory. She has waited long enough. It is her time now.

Her parents are pleased, though they want to know why one grade was lower than the rest and whose fault it is. Was the teaching not up to scratch? Probably, they agree. But the letter confirming her place at university comes two days later and within a month, her suitcase is packed and her bank account opened in her own name and she has her birth certificate and her papers and she is escaping.

At the station, her mam buys them both a large whiskey in the buffet bar.

They both know she will not be back. Carrie hugs her. She has paid her debts, honoured her father and mother. She imagines she is free.

How wrong she is.

As she walks out to the platform, she tells her mam, quietly, that her granda used to 'touch me, you know'.

Her mam says why didn't she say something?

Carrie says how could she have?

Her mam reminds her that it happens to most girls growing up and to put it behind her and not be silly and for God's sake, she's a grown woman now. Get over it.

Chapter 15

The Present

HAVE I REGRETS?

The counsellor's question makes me pause for a moment. I want to answer her as honestly as I can, for she is doing her best for me. I reckon I would win my court case even without her report, because, as countless psychiatrists and professionals have told me over the years, Public Carrie presents well. But she is trying to help us both. Public Carrie and Private Carrie. Public Carrie is a mistress of disguise, of dissembling. That's what enabled her to stay in overdrive for so long, covertly self-medicating, vomiting, bleeding. Public Carrie is the one my family are proud of, who has done so well, who has achieved so much, who has been a good daughter. Public Carrie would never go into therapy. I tell the counsellor they believe that all she needs to do is stop wallowing in the past. In her own misery and self-pity. Eat properly. Get enough sleep. Put the cork in the bottle. Plenty of others have done it. Look at her granda.

When I explain this, my counsellor wonders aloud if I feel hurt. Betrayed. But I don't. I don't get angry. I shy away from confrontation. I retreat into my head.

She tells me I am a textbook case, ticking all the boxes on her questionnaire – dysfunctional and/or violent relationships? Check. Eating disorders, substance abuse, self-harming, dependency on prescription drugs? Check. She expresses incredulity at what I was prescribed as a teenager – *did my parents not wonder?*

I will never know, for I can never ask them. I have done the unspeakable. I have told my secret.

Soon I will go to court. And I will be believed. Granda is long dead. Craig is dead many years, too, from pancreatic cancer at thirty-seven. The police have no possibility of a prosecution. As so often in retrospective cases, they are not involved. That doesn't matter, I tell the counsellor, and it is the truth. My truth. It is not closure, but it will be as close to it as I get in this life.

In time, I shall wean myself from my last guilty pleasure. Even now, I am becoming selective. I only attend court for retrospective cases. I like ones where I can find little parallels: a date, a year, a family member, even the most passing reference to a pigeon club secures my attention. It gives me a sense of identification, of belonging. Sometimes, in the lobby or the coffee bar or the toilets, I make eye contact with a survivor. I like to think we recognise each other by some unspoken signal. Something subliminal that says, 'I've been there, too.' Whimsically, I imagine I can send them strength to help them tell their truth.

Most days now, I may be reasonably happy. It's a strange feeling. I'm not a good person. I can forgive but I can't forget. The dead still walk with me. What happened in that pigeon loft will shadow my waking hours and trouble my dreams until I die. Then, I know now, it will die with me. The child that is growing inside me tells me that. My child will be my revenge, laughing and living far from my world where, it seems, it is still the dead who kill the living.